Many mother animals feed their young with their own milk and bring them up with loving care. A baby animal follows its mother around and learns many things. In the wild, if the baby animal leaves its mother's side and gets lost, it is almost certain to die. When attacked by other animals, the mother and baby must flee together.

At times, in order to protect her baby, the mother will charge at an animal stronger than herself. A mother defending her baby becomes very strong. A mother rhinoceros or water buffalo will chase away lions without a moment's hesitation. Even animals that are thought to be weaker, such as antelope, zebras, giraffes, and ostriches, will give chase to animals that threaten their young. There are few examples in nature more powerful than a mother animal protecting her offspring.

RHINOCEROS MOTHER

written and illustrated by *Toshi Yoshida*

PHILOMEL BOOKS
New York

On the African plain, a mother rhinoceros stands with her baby in the hot sun of midday. The mother rhinoceros has been wounded; her side is bleeding.

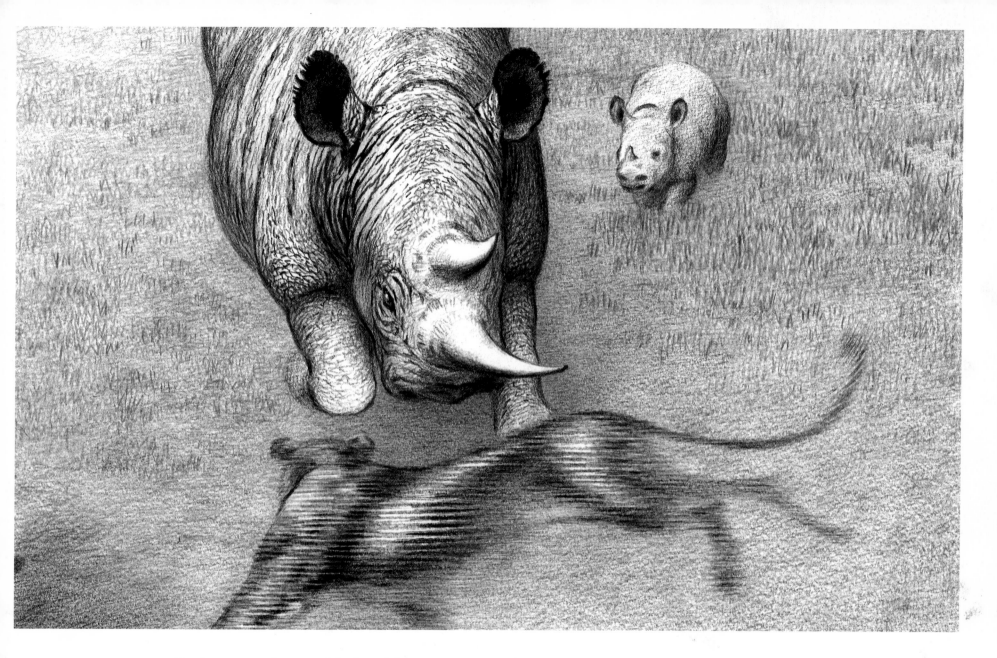

Perhaps mother and baby rhinoceros met a lion.
No, a mother rhinoceros will charge at any animal that might endanger her baby,
and a lion would run away.

Perhaps they met a male rhinoceros. His horn would wound her.
But it isn't likely a male rhinoceros would charge a female rhinoceros.

Oryx, members of the antelope family, have pointed horns as sharp as spears.
But they are grass-eating animals. They would never charge a rhinoceros.

The only animals in the area that could wound a rhinoceros so badly
are water buffalo and elephants.

But why would a water buffalo or an elephant quarrel with a rhinoceros?
Generally, they stay with their own kind.

The actual adventure began in the morning. Mother and baby rhinoceros set off in search of some delicious grass. Four tickbirds perched on mother's back.

They passed giraffes eating leaves from the trees and watching the rhinoceroses as they wandered off onto the plain.

Finally, mother and baby rhinoceros stopped to eat some delicious green grass.
In a nearby forest, a herd of eleven elephants were eating leaves.

Before long, a baby boy elephant came out of the forest
and onto the plain. He thought the baby rhinoceros was a baby elephant,
and was coming to take a look at him.

The two baby animals approached each other with curiosity.
The baby elephant touched baby rhinoceros's face with his trunk.
Baby rhinoceros's ears were very small and strange.

For a nose, he had no long trunk, but just two holes. Above them,
a bit of a horn was sticking out.
Mother rhinoceros thought baby elephant might hurt her calf.

She came charging angrily.
Baby elephant was taken by surprise and jumped aside.
The birds on mother rhinoceros's back flew up all at once.

Mother elephant, who had come to fetch baby elephant,
thought *he* was in danger. She came charging at mother rhinoceros.

Finally, mother and baby rhinoceros ran away. The four tickbirds
settled on mother's back, the same as always.

Mother and baby elephant returned to the forest where the rest
of the herd was waiting for them.

The wounded mother rhinoceros walked home slowly and painfully across the golden plain. What a terrible thing had happened.

The giraffes looked out from the woods at the two passing rhinoceroses.
They couldn't see the wound on mother rhinoceros's side,
but they could smell the blood.

At last, mother and baby rhinoceros came home to the woods where
they live. Their adventure was over.

Now mother rhinoceros is standing very still. Baby rhinoceros looks worried, but he doesn't know what to do.

Evening comes. Mother rhinoceros's wound hurts and she can't move.

If the wound gets infected, she will probably die. Baby rhinoceros can
do nothing for her.

Night comes to an end, and the sun begins to spread its light
across the plain.

Some giraffes walk slowly through the woods.

The red light of dawn makes the plain near the woods glow.
It turns mother rhinoceros a soft red. After a long night,
mother rhinoceros finally begins to feel much better.

The four tickbirds on her back busily eat horseflies and ticks
from around her wound, protecting mother rhinoceros from sickness.

Soon, mother rhinoceros is completely well. She and baby rhinoceros
walk toward the river to take a bath. Crowned cranes, saddle-billed storks,
and sacred ibis wade nearby.

Some cattle egrets have come for a drink. None of the birds are afraid
of mother and baby rhinoceros.
Today, the four tickbirds have flown elsewhere, but soon they will
return to perch on mother rhinoceros's back, as always.

Tickbirds are similar to starlings. Perching on the backs of animals such as rhinoceroses, water buffalo, hippopotamuses, giraffes, and antelope, they eat ticks and other insects, helping to keep the animals clean and free from disease. They always settle on the same animal, and when danger approaches, they fly around crying loudly in warning. In this way, different species of animals live together and help one another.

English language translation copyright © 1991 by Susan Matsui.
Original edition copyright © 1984 by Toshi Yoshida.
English translation rights arranged with Fukutake Publishing, Co., Ltd.,
through Japan Foreign Rights Centre.
First American edition published in 1991 by
Philomel Books, a division of The Putnam & Grosset Book Group,
200 Madison Avenue, New York, NY 10016.   Originally published in Japanese in 1984
by Fukutake Publishing Co., Ltd., Tokyo, under the title *Kanchigai*.
Published simultaneously in Canada.
Printed in Hong Kong by South China Printing Co. (1988) Ltd.

Library of Congress Cataloging-in-Publication Data   Yoshida, Toshi, 1911-   Rhinoceros
Mother   Translation from the Japanese. Summary: Illustrates how animals help each
other in nature and protect their young. 1. Mutualism (Biology)—Juvenile literature.
2. Parental behavior in animals—Juvenile literature. [1. Symbiosis. 2. Parental behavior
in animals. 3. Animals—Habits and behavior] I. Title. QH548.3.Y67   1991   591.51
90-7452   ISBN 0-399-22270-7

First Impression